The Pout-Pout Fish

Deborah Diesen

Pictures by Dan Hanna

Farrar Straus Giroux
New York

For Mason and Isaac
—D.D.

For Stella
—D.H.

Text copyright © 2008 by Deborah Diesen
Pictures copyright © 2008 by Dan Hanna
Color separations by Chroma Graphics PTE Ltd.
Printed in China by South China Printing Co.,
Dongguan City, Guangdong Province
Designed by Jay Colvin
First hardcover edition, 2008
10 9 8 7 6 5 4 3 2 1

www.fsgkidsbooks.com

Library of Congress Cataloging-in-Publication Data
Diesen, Deborah.
    The pout-pout fish / Deborah Diesen ; pictures by Dan Hanna.— 1st ed.
        p. cm.
    Summary: The pout-pout fish believes he only knows how to frown, even though
many of his friends suggest ways to change his expression, until one day a fish comes
along that shows him otherwise.
    ISBN 978-0-374-36096-2
    [1. Fishes—Fiction.   2. Marine animals—Fiction.   3. Friendship—Fiction.
4. Attitude (Psychology)—Fiction.   5. Stories in rhyme.] I. Hanna, Dan, ill.
II. Title.

PZ8.3.D565 Po 2008
[Fic]—dc21

                                                    2007060730

ISBN 978-0-374-36098-6

This special edition was printed for Kohl's Department Stores, Inc.
(for distribution on behalf of Kohl's Cares, LLC, its wholly owned subsidiary)
by Farrar Straus Giroux Books for Young Readers.
978-0-374-36098-6 • Kohl's • 0-374-36098-7 • 123386 • 1/13–3/13

Deep in the water
Where the fish hang out
Lives a glum gloomy swimmer
With an ever-present pout.

"I'm a *pout-pout* fish
With a *pout-pout* face,
So I spread the dreary-wearies
All over the place."

BLUB

BLUUUB

BLUUUUUUUUB

Along comes a clam
With a wide winning grin
And a pearl of advice
For her pal to take in:

"Hey, Mr. Fish,
With your crosstown frown,
Don't you think it's time to
Turn it upside down?"

Says the fish to his friend,
"Nice thought, Ms. Clam.
I hear what you're saying,
But it's just the way I am.

"I'm a *pout-pout* fish
With a *pout-pout* face,
So I spread the dreary-wearies
All over the place."

Along comes a jellyfish.
He floats through the ocean,
His tentacles all trailing
In a gentle locomotion.

"Hey, Mr. Fish,
With your daily scaly scowl,
I wish you wouldn't greet us
With a grimace and a growl."

Says the fish to his friend,
"Mr. Jelly, I agree.
I'd like to be more friendly,
But it isn't up to me.

"I'm a *pout-pout* fish
With a *pout-pout* face,
So I spread the dreary-wearies
All over the place."

BLUB

BLUUUB

BLUUUUUB

Along comes a squid,
Quite a slender squiggly sight.
She is squirmy, she is squelchy,
She is slightly impolite.

"Hey, Mr. Fish,
You kaleidoscope of mope,
How about a smile?
A little joy? A little hope?"

Says the fish to his friend,
"Mrs. Squid, I would try,
But I haven't any choice.
Take a look and you'll see why.

"I'm a *pout-pout* fish
With a *pout-pout* face,
So I spread the dreary-wearies
All over the place."

Along comes an octopus
With eight great arms
Covered on the underside
With tiny sucker charms.

"Hey, Mr. Fish,
Let me tell it to you straight.
Your hulky-bulky sulking
Is an unattractive trait!"

Says the fish to his friend,
"Mr. Eight, my chum,
With a mouth like mine
I am *destined* to be glum.

"I'm a *pout-pout* fish
With a *pout-pout* face,
So I spread the dreary-wearies
All over the place."

Now along comes a fish
In a silent silver shimmer.
The gang has never seen before
This bright and brilliant swimmer.

She approaches Mr. Fish,
But instead of saying hey . . .

She plants a kiss upon his pout
And then she swims
Away.

Mr. Fish is most astounded.
Mr. Fish is just aghast.
He is stone-faced like a statue.
Then he blinks, and speaks at last:

"My friends," says Mr. Fish,
"I should have known it all along.
I thought that I was pouty,
But it turns out I was wrong.

"I'm a *kiss-kiss* fish
With a *kiss-kiss* face

For spreading cheery-cheeries
All over the place!"

So I'll . . .

Smooch

Smooch

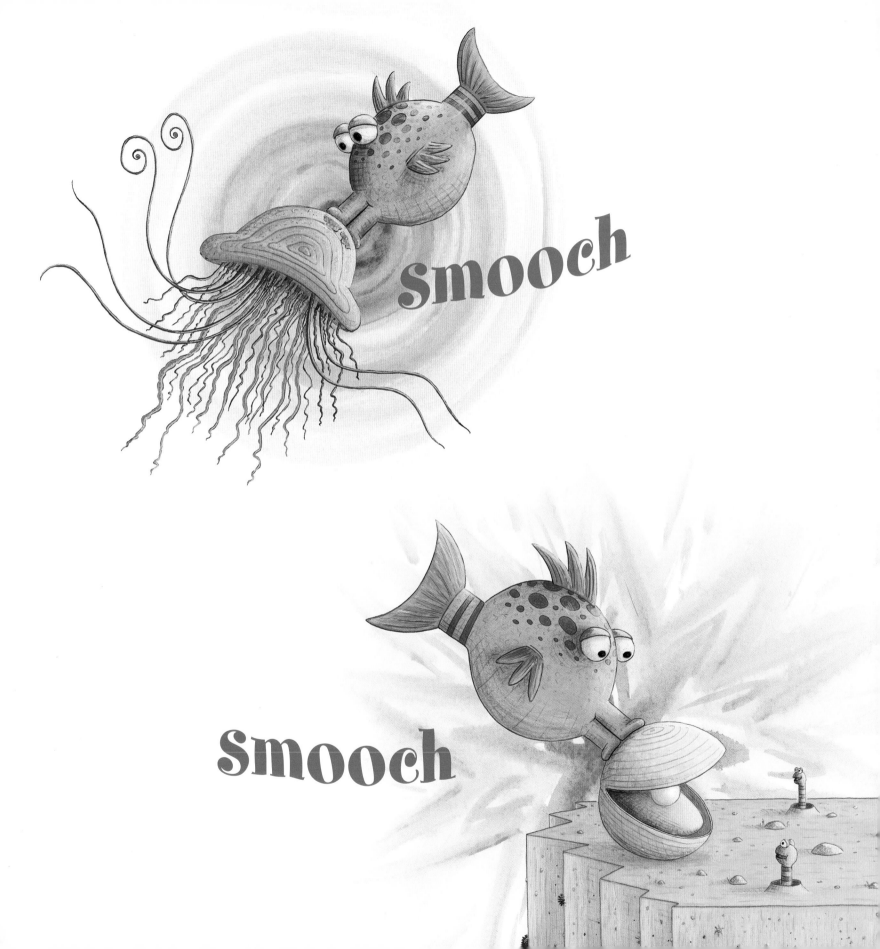

Smooch

Smooch

SMOOOOOOOOOCH!